Howard's House is Haunted

Have you read these Shooting Star books?

- ❏ *Aliens in the Basement* • Suzan Reid
- ❏ *The Big Race!* • Sylvia McNicoll
- ❏ *A Ghost in the Attic* • Suzan Reid
- ❏ *Liar, Liar, Pants on Fire* • Gordon Korman
- ❏ *The Lost Locket* • Carol Matas
- ❏ *Monsters in the School* • Martyn Godfrey
- ❏ *Princesses Don't Wear Jeans* • Brenda Bellingham
- ❏ *Project Disaster* • Sylvia McNicoll
- ❏ *School Campout* • Becky Citra
- ❏ *Sleepover Zoo* • Brenda Kearns
- ❏ *Starring Me!* • Cathy Miyata
- ❏ *Wonder Dog* • Beverly Scudamore
- ❏ *Worm Pie* • Beverly Scudamore

Howard's House is Haunted

Maureen Bayless

Illustrations by
Janet Wilson

Scholastic Canada Ltd.

Canadian Cataloguing in Publication Data

Bayless, Maureen
    Howard's house is haunted

(Shooting Star)
ISBN 0-590-74559-X

I. Title.   II. Series.
PS8553.A94H69 1993   jC813'.54   C92-095361-1
PZ7.B39Ho 1993

10 9 8 7 6   Printed in Canada   9 / 9 0 1 2 3 / 0

For
Schmoo, Yaki and Bean
because of
Grammy, Poppa and Gumba.

Contents

Chapter 1

Howard the Coward

Howard was a coward. And everybody knew it.

Howard was afraid of ghosts, spiders, creaky noises, slithery snakes, bullies, basements, and the dark. He was afraid of lots of things. Almost everything, in fact.

Since Howard was a coward, you can imagine how he felt when his parents told him they had bought a haunted house.

"We've finally got our own house, dear," Howard's mother said one evening. "No more apartments for us."

1

Howard was eating green noodles with cheese sauce, his favourite. He was slurping them up his chin and pretending he was a lawnmower.

"Mm-r-r-r-r," he said, snipping the green noodles with his teeth. He didn't care about houses.

"I think you'll like this house, Howie," said Howard's father, pouring him a glass of Orange Fizzie. "It's really big. And it's really old. It's got turrets and trap doors and twenty-nine rooms."

"Yeah?" Howard pushed his nose across his plate. He was down to the short noodles.

"You probably know the house. It's the big brown one on Walnut Street. The one with the long grass."

"Not that one!" said Howard. "Not the brown one on Walnut Street! Not the one with the crooked chimney and creaky gate! Not the one with the super-high hedge! It's haunted! Everybody knows that!"

Howard's father laughed. "Yes, we heard. That's why we got such a good deal on it."

"A deal! Who cares about a deal?" yelled Howard. "There's a ghost in that house! I'm not moving in with any ghost."

"I thought you didn't believe in ghosts," murmured Howard's mother, flipping through a copy of the magazine she worked for.

"Witches," groaned Howard. "I don't believe in *witches*."

He hadn't believed scary stories about witches since Mrs. Merrymore next door had told him she was a witch. Mrs. Merrymore didn't wear a pointy hat, ride a broom or live with a black cat. And she made wonderful chocolate chip soup. Howard only believed in good witches now.

Howard's mother cleared her throat. "Well, the best thing about this house is that it's big enough that Gramma can live with us."

Gramma Brady was getting old. If she didn't come to live with Howard's family, she'd have to go to an old folks' home.

Howard thought about that. He didn't want Gramma to live in an old folks' home. But he didn't want to live with a ghost, either.

"Maybe you can send me to boarding school," he suggested.

"No way," said Dad.

"Maybe I can join the army."

"Right," said Dad. "In about ten years."

Howard looked at the last noodles lying on his plate. They looked as sad as he felt.

"Know any good jails that take kids?" he mumbled.

"Howard," said Mom, sternly.

"Yeah?"

"Stop moping and do the dishes."

Howard stomped out of the kitchen. "We won't last a night in that haunted house," he fumed. "And I'm not going to spend what's left of my life washing dishes."

"Look, Howard." Dad smiled. "If we get scared to death, then we'll be ghosts, too. And we ghosts might need some ghostly dishes."

Howard didn't think Dad was very funny. As he dabbed away at the stack of dishes, he tried to think of a way to keep his parents from moving into that house.

Or else to get the ghost to move out.

Because there was one thing Howard knew absolutely for sure. There was no way he was going to sleep in the same house as a ghost. Even if that house had turrets, trap doors, and twenty-nine rooms.

Especially if that house had twenty-nine rooms.

An awful lot of creaky noises could come out of twenty-nine rooms.

Chapter 2

Moving Day

On Monday, the moving van came and took all the Bradys' furniture to their new house. Their new haunted house.

Mom told Howard he could stay home from school and help move.

"No way," Howard said. "I've got to fix this thing, and fast."

And he dashed off to school. Just to be safe, he carried all his favourite things with him. Scruffy Monkey, which had slept with him since he was a baby. His posters. His wood chisels and pocket knife and the things he had

carved with them. His Porky Pig flashlight. And his fluorescent dominoes.

He wasn't taking any chances on the ghost getting those.

Howard ran around the playground at school until he spotted two of his friends. They were jumping in a pile of raked leaves and kicking them across the grass.

When they noticed Howard with his bag of stuff, they gathered around him.

"Is that for Show and Tell?" asked Rebecca Green.

"The toy bank?" wondered Willie Wong.

Howard told them about his problem.

"Get out of here," laughed Willie. "Your parents wouldn't buy a haunted house. You're just worried about nothing, as usual."

"No, really," said Howard. "It's the brown house on Walnut Street."

His friends stopped laughing.

"I know that one," said Rebecca. "Sometimes, when I'm walking home from my clarinet lesson, I see lights flickering in the top windows.

But nobody lives there!"

"I wouldn't want to be in your shoes," said Willie.

Just then, the bell rang.

Howard walked off to class, clutching Scruffy Monkey to his chest. The hair stood up on the back of his head. He felt almost as if the ghost's ghoulish eyes were watching him.

Watching and waiting.

In class, Howard could hardly keep his mind on the arithmetic questions Miss Bruce was writing on the board. He kept wondering whether the ghost was, right that minute, trying out his bed.

A wet paper ball hit him in the head and fell onto his desk.

Howard opened it.

There was a drawing of him holding Scruffy Monkey.

Underneath it, in black, black pencil, was written: "What's the matter, Fraidy Brady???? So chicken you gotta bring your dolly to school?"

On the other side, the wet side, was another note. "Howard the coward is so chicken he asks his mummy before he pees his pants."

There was a mean snicker from the other side of the room.

Howard looked across to the big, freckled face of the class bully, Punch McLaredy.

Punch pointed to Scruffy Monkey. Then he picked an imaginary monkey from his own lap, held it out in front of him, and gave it several loud, smacking kisses.

Miss Bruce didn't notice. Her chalk was squeaking.

But the other kids saw. Some of them began to giggle. None of them knew about Howard's ghost.

But even if they did know, thought Howard, they probably wouldn't care. Probably none of them was afraid of ghosts. Only Howard was. Everybody knew he was a coward.

When I die, thought Howard, they're going to write on my tombstone, "Howard the Coward. He lived. He feared. And he died."

Howard sniffed a little. He wanted to cry. Instead, he just pretended he had a cold.

Then a thought struck him.

Howard looked over at Punch.

Punch leered back and pretended to rock a baby.

"Frank!" said Miss Bruce sharply, using Punch's real name. "I'll be collecting homework in five minutes. I hope your dog hasn't eaten yours."

Punch stuck his tongue out at Miss Bruce's back.

Punch, thought Howard, you are a real creep.

But if anybody could scare a ghost out of a house, a creep could. And Punch was just the creep to do it.

Chapter 3

Truce

There was one big problem with Howard's plan. The ghost might be afraid of Punch. But so was Howard.

All morning, Howard thought about Punch. He thought about how big he was. He thought about how mean he was. He thought about how nobody, not even the big kids, talked to Punch unless they had to.

But all morning, Howard also thought about the ghost. The ghost who was waiting for him at home.

At recess, Howard screwed up what little

courage he had. He tiptoed up to Punch in the playground.

"Truce," Howard croaked.

Punch looked surprised. He also looked like he couldn't decide whether to hit Howard or not.

"Say the magic words," he snarled.

Howard had been practising. He'd never had to say them before, because he'd never had to talk to Punch before.

"Truce, truce, break a truce, stand on your head and kiss Miss Bruce," squeaked Howard.

Punch cocked an eyebrow.

"Now lick sand," he ordered.

Howard thought about how much he needed Punch's help. He walked over to the swings, bent down, and stuck the tip of his tongue in the sand.

He walked back to Punch and showed him his tongue.

"Okay, shoot," said Punch. "What's up?"

Howard tried to tell him, but he couldn't talk very well with his tongue sticking out.

"Wha thould I do with the thand?" asked

Howard. He wasn't sure if he was allowed to wipe it off.

"I dunno," replied Punch. "Nobody's ever actually done it before."

Howard wiped his tongue on his sleeve.

He told Punch about the house on Walnut Street.

Punch gave him a long look.

"I know that house," he said. "I knocked on the door one Halloween and a spooky voice said, 'Go-o-o a-wa-a-ay, Pu-unch!'"

"The ghost knew your name!" breathed Howard. This was one smart ghost.

"Yup," said Punch. "I broke a window there once. Probably remembered me from then. I wouldn't want to be you, that's for sure."

Howard wished he hadn't left Scruffy Monkey on his chair. He could really use him to hang on to right now.

"I need your help, Punch," he said desperately. "I need you to get rid of this ghost for me."

Punch laughed. It was a short, loud, rude laugh.

"Help you!" he sneered. "Why should I help a chicken yo-yo like you? What's in it for me?"

Good question. What was in it for Punch? Howard thought.

"I'll lend you my Porky Pig flashlight," he suggested hopefully.

Punch hooted.

"My fluorescent dominoes?" Howard offered.

Punch laughed so hard he nearly fell over. Everyone in the playground looked at them.

"Well, what then?" scowled Howard. He couldn't bring himself to offer Scruffy Monkey. And he had an idea Scruffy Monkey wouldn't go over too well, either.

Punch hiccupped, holding his belly. He shrugged and turned to go.

Then he stopped. He turned back to Howard.

"There is one thing," he said slyly.

"What?" Howard asked quickly.

"My homework. Promise you'll do my homework for me, and I'll help," said Punch. He looked sideways at Howard.

"We're not allowed to — "

Punch shrugged and turned his back again.

Howard watched him walk away. He got as far as the swings. Then the slide. Then the monkey bars.

"All right!" cried Howard. "I'll do it."

Punch came back, grinning.

"It's not much anyway," said Howard. "Only a story report."

Punch leered. "I didn't mean just today's homework," he said. "I meant for life. And you promised!"

Howard swallowed.

"Okay," he gulped. After all, what did it matter if he got expelled for doing Punch's homework? Expelled was better than dead. And if Punch didn't scare away that ghost. . . .

Punch looked pleased. He picked up a stone and rubbed it between his fingers thoughtfully. After a minute, he threw the stone at the swings. It pinged off the top bar.

"Here's the plan," he said, just as the bell rang. "People are afraid of snakes, aren't they? And ghosts are just dead people. So maybe ghosts are afraid of snakes, too!"

"Yeah?" said Howard uncertainly.

"So," said Punch, "I'll lend you my pet snake, Chokey."

Howard's heart did a jump. It might work! There was just one thing.

"I'm afraid of snakes," he whispered. "You bring it."

Punch made a rude noise. Then he leaned toward Howard.

"All right, I'll bring him," said Punch. "But you'd better do a good job on my homework, hear? I want old Bruce-beak off my back!"

Howard hurried back to the classroom and squeezed Scruffy Monkey into his desk.

He felt much better.

It was worth getting sand and sweater fuzz on his tongue to get Punch's help. It was even worth doing two sets of homework for the rest of his life.

At least, he hoped it was.

Chapter 4

The House on Walnut Street

When Howard and Punch walked up to the house on Walnut Street that afternoon, the moving van was just leaving.

Mom was leaning over the tippy fence, talking to an old woman who was wearing galoshes and leaning on a cane.

"Hello, Howard. Hello, Frank," said Mom. "I was just getting to know our new neighbour, Mrs. Nutt."

Mrs. Nutt squinted at the two boys.

"Keep your toys, dogs, bikes and feet out of my yard," she said. Then she winked. Or

19

maybe she just blinked.

"I wonder how she feels about snakes?" said Punch as they went up the sagging steps. His pet boa, Chokey, was in his backpack.

His homework was in Howard's backpack.

As they crossed the front porch, Howard heard Mrs. Nutt say to his mother, "You're a brave woman, Charlene. I wouldn't live in that old house if you paid me a million dollars. You never know what might happen."

The big double door creaked on its ancient hinges as Punch pushed it open.

Inside was a wide hallway and a curving staircase with a step missing. Wallpaper was hanging off the wall in strips. A chandelier tied in a plastic bag swung above them.

"Wow!" exclaimed Punch. "This could be a ghost *hotel!*"

Dad came into the hallway with a bucket and mop. His head was wrapped in a kerchief.

"Wear a hat in here, boys," he said, sloshing water onto the floor. "There's spiderwebs everywhere."

"Ugh! Gross!" cried Howard. He hated spiders. They scared him.

Dad flicked the mop into the air, then plopped it into the puddle. "We'll have this place spanking clean in no time. Just needs a bit of elbow grease. You'll see," he said. "In two weeks, Gramma will be able to move in."

Dad told Howard his room would be on the second floor, in the front turret.

Howard remembered the ghostly lights Rebecca had seen.

"What room are those top windows in?" he asked.

Dad scratched his kerchief.

"I believe those are the attic windows," he said. "Trouble is, we haven't found a way in yet. There should be an opening somewhere, but we haven't found it yet. Maybe the windows are just for show."

Howard shivered. Not just for show, he thought. Just for ghosts. And his room would be right under the ghost's.

Where the tread was missing on the staircase,

Dad had taped a sign that said, Watch Your Step! The boys hopped over it. Howard hoped Dad would fix it soon. The hole was scary.

They found Howard's room at the top of the tower. His bed and dresser were already in it.

There was a water stain on the wooden floor below the window. The window had a patch over one pane.

"Bull's-eye!" whooped Punch. He grinned proudly. "There wouldn't be one window left in this place if that ghost hadn't — "

Howard cleared his throat.

"Speaking of ghosts," he said, tossing his backpack on the bed. Punch put his pack on a pillow so that Chokey would be comfortable. Then they set off to explore the house.

They discovered a small door in Howard's closet which led to another bedroom. In that bedroom was another closet, which also led to a bedroom. By walking through closets, they could circle through all six bedrooms and the bathroom on the second floor without even using the hallway!

They found two trap doors, too, but neither led to the attic. One was really a laundry chute. The other was a coal chute in the basement.

"Bummer," said Punch. "These aren't any fun."

Howard could tell by the furniture that Gramma was going to sleep in the room next to his. On the other side of his room was Mom's writing room, where she would do her magazine work, and next to that was his parents' bedroom.

"Nobody's going to be near me until Gramma comes. And that's not for two weeks," he said to Punch. "I don't think I'll live that long."

Punch didn't look too concerned about that.

"Let's get started," he said. "First, we'll take Chokey through every room so the ghost is sure to see him. Then we'll figure out where the ghost camps out and leave the snake there, in a box. A few days should do it."

Punch untied the string on his knapsack flap and reached in. He frowned and patted around. Chokey was gone. A flap might keep rain out of a pack, but it obviously couldn't keep snakes in!

"Oh, no!" Howard yelled, jumping onto his dresser. If there was one thing as scary as ghosts, it was snakes.

Punch looked everywhere. No Chokey.

"He could be anywhere," he said. "He curls up really small." Punch looked as if he was going to cry.

Which was very strange, thought Howard. Bullies don't cry.

"As soon as he shows up, I'll call you," said Howard, trying to sound comforting. "He can't be far. But, Punch — "

"Yeah?"

"Will he eat me?"

Punch hooted. "Get real. Why would any snake want to eat a nerd like you?"

Howard didn't feel better at all.

"Ease up," said Punch. "Don't call the pound. Chokey won't be hungry for at least a week. And if he's got any taste at all, he'll go for a rat."

Howard brightened. "Or a ghost. Maybe he'll think ghosts are a real delicacy."

Howard hoped Chokey had slithered into the attic. The ghost might be packing his bags right now.

He didn't think he'd mention Chokey to his mom, though. She probably had enough on her mind right now.

Chapter 5

Creak, Creak, Thud

That night, Howard dreaded going to bed.

First, he did two sets of homework.

He did them very slowly. He even typed Punch's. Since he didn't know how to type, that took a very long time.

"That's my boy," said his father, walking by with a ladder.

Howard asked his parents if he could sleep with them, but they said they were going to stay up late, wallpapering.

He didn't think he wanted to stay in their

room by himself. It was even bigger and creakier than his.

He settled for curling up with Scruffy Monkey, and he hoped that Chokey was curled up asleep somewhere, too. Somewhere far away.

He could hear his dad whistling and his mother humming below him. Soon, even though he thought it would never happen, he was fast asleep.

In the middle of the night he woke up.

He thought he heard something.

Creak. Creak. Thud. Creak. Creak.

He definitely heard something.

Howard jumped out of bed and raced to his parents' room, sure every step of the way that the ghost was going to grab him.

"Mom! Dad!" he called.

"M-mm?" his mother answered.

"The ghost! I heard the ghost!" Howard leaped onto his parents' bed and threw himself between them.

"Howie! Get off! We just got to sleep!" his father said crankily.

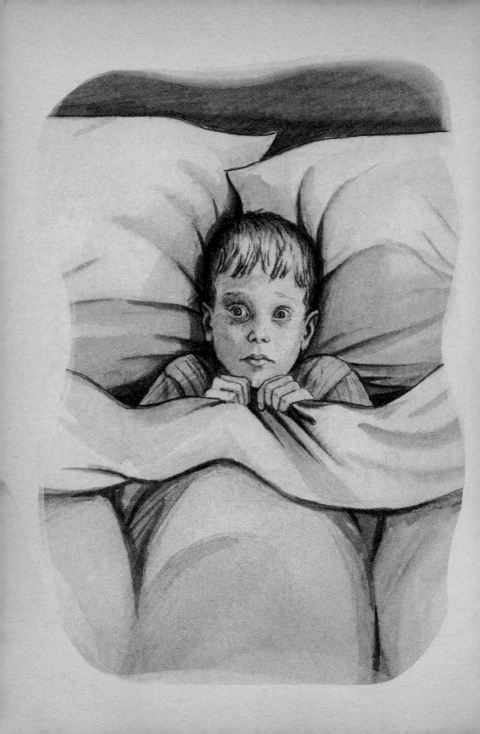

"But I heard the ghost! He was creaking!"

"Howie, there's no such thing as a ghost. Can't you pretend it's a witch, instead?" sighed his mother, not opening her eyes.

"The least you can do, Howie, is lie still. We can't sleep with all your bouncing," muttered Dad.

That's what Howard did. He lay still, right in between his parents. He felt much less scared. He wished he'd brought Scruffy Monkey, though.

In the morning, there was proof that the ghost had visited. The leftover pizza they had put in the fridge was gone.

Eaten.

The last bottle of Orange Fizzie was sitting on the counter.

Empty.

And Howard's pot of chocolate chip soup, a moving gift from Mrs. Merrymore, was missing entirely.

"Howard!" said Mom, hands on her hips.

"I told you there was a ghost," said Howard.

"You're the ghost," said Mom.

"No wonder you had nightmares," said Dad, shaking his head.

"No dessert for the day," said Mom, crossly.

Howard stomped up to his room.

"Hey ghost!" he yelled, looking up at the ceiling. "Bring back my chocolate chip soup!"

At school, he consulted Punch.

"Must have been the ghost," agreed Punch. "Chokey doesn't like Orange Fizzie."

"What'll I do?" asked Howard.

"Buy a chocolate bar from the machine."

"No, I mean about the ghost!"

"Oh," said Punch. He swung his knapsack around for a moment. "How's this. Ghosts come out at night, right?"

"Right."

"That must mean they don't like light, right?"

"Right," said Howard. "So?"

"Well," said Punch. "Why don't you leave all the lights on? All night. Pretty soon, that ghost will find himself another hotel. What with all those lights and Chokey kicking around."

Howard thought it was a great idea.

Of course, his parents wouldn't let him leave all the lights on.

"Are you crazy?" asked Mom. "Don't you know what electricity costs?" And she shook her head over him like he was going bananas.

That night, after doing two sets of homework, he lay in bed until his parents were asleep.

Then, carrying Scruffy Monkey, he tiptoed through the house and turned all the lights on. Even the lights over the front and back porches. Even the light over Mom's typewriter.

While he was at it, he looked for Chokey. Punch was pretty worried about that snake. And Howard was even more worried — but for different reasons.

No Chokey.

When he woke up, all the lights were off.

He did the same thing Wednesday night, Thursday night, and Friday night.

And each morning the lights were off.

Saturday morning there was a note taped to his backpack.

It said:

Power is expensive. Have you gone crazy?

Signed, the ghost.

Chapter 6

Get That Ghost!

All Saturday morning, Howard wished he could go to Punch's house and show him the note.

But all Saturday morning, he had to pull weeds out of the front yard.

He couldn't even show the note to his parents. They'd think he'd written it himself. And he'd have to explain why he'd been turning all the lights on.

Sometimes parents were more trouble than they were worth.

Mrs. Nutt hung her head out of one of her windows.

"Keep those weeds away from my yard!" she called. "They're catching."

Yup, his parents had picked a winner of a house, all right. Great yard. Great ghost. Great neighbours, too.

Just then, Punch wheeled up on his ancient bike.

"Found my snake yet?" he asked, hopping off.

Howard shook his head.

"But look at this," he said, showing Punch the note.

"Holy macaroni," Punch said, sitting down.

One good thing about Punch, thought Howard. He might be a bully. But he believes you.

"This is war," said Punch.

"War," agreed Howard.

They pulled weeds together for a while, thinking.

"What do we know about this ghost?" asked

Punch. Howard thought. "We know that he likes pizza, Orange Fizzie, and chocolate chip soup. He creaks. He writes. And he can turn off lights."

"And I think he's got Chokey. So he's probably not afraid of snakes," added Punch.

He probably *eats* snakes, thought Howard. But he didn't say that.

They mulled this information over.

"There must be some way we can use what we know about him to get that ghost," said Punch. "I want my snake back."

"I put up a sign on the fridge yesterday," said Howard. "But my mom ripped it down."

The sign had said 'No gohsts aloud.' His mother had made him wash the tape marks off the fridge.

"But there must be something," said Punch. "Something sure-fire and foolproof."

"Maybe there is," said Howard, getting an idea. "Tell me that tapeworm joke you told the class once."

"Why?"

"Just tell it."

Punch scratched his head. "I'm not sure I remember it," he said, "but it went something like this:

"A guy goes to the doctor 'cause he's not feeling well. He's eating lots but he's getting skinnier and skinnier.

"The doctor tells him he's got a tapeworm. The tapeworm is eating all his food.

"The doctor tells the guy to eat a raisin cookie and a popsicle every three hours and come back in a week.

"The guy doesn't know why, but he does it. So he comes back in a week.

"The doctor tells the guy to eat the cookie, like always. But not to eat the popsicle.

"The guy does it. They wait a few minutes.

"Then the tapeworm sticks his head out and yells, 'Hey, where's my popsicle?' And the doctor bops it on the head."

Howard shook his head. "That's really gross," he groaned.

"Yeah, well, I guess," said Punch. "But how

can it help? You don't have a tapeworm."

"No," said Howard. "But I have a ghost. A ghost who likes chocolate chip soup. And Orange Fizzie."

"So?"

"So," grinned Howard, bending near Punch so that the ghost, if he was near, couldn't hear. "So, we put out a bowl of chocolate chip soup and a bottle of Orange Fizzie every night. And then one night we just put out the soup and —"

"And boppo-kaplow, we get him," shouted Punch. "And if he doesn't cough Chokey up, he'll be sorry!"

"Right," said Howard.

He didn't want to think too much about the second part. The getting part. He hoped Punch would handle that.

Chapter 7

The Trap

As soon as the weeding was done, Howard biked over to Mrs. Merrymore's apartment and asked her for her soup recipe.

"It's easy," said Mrs. Merrymore when Howard had explained what he needed it for. "Besides my secret ingredients, which I'll give to you, all you need are chocolate chips and a stove. Do you have those things?"

"Can I use a microwave?" asked Howard. He wasn't allowed to use the stove yet.

"I think so," smiled Mrs. Merrymore. "But I've never heard of a haunted house with a microwave oven in it! Didn't think ghosts went for those sorts of modern things."

She gave Howard a vial of secret formula and let him mix up a batch of chocolate chip soup right there, for practice.

"Smells like peppermint," said Howard, sniffing the vial.

"Might be," said Mrs. Merrymore, her eyes twinkling. "Or it might be the juice of goblin mushrooms, picked at midnight."

Howard looked at her. "So long as it's not lizard tails or spider legs or anything like that," he said. Sometimes he forgot about Mrs. Merrymore being a witch.

"Absolutely not," agreed Mrs. Merrymore. "I'm strictly a vegetarian sort of witch."

Howard couldn't wait to try his plan.

"Well, thanks!" he said. Then he hopped onto his bike and pedalled for home.

That night, Howard worked late, cutting pictures of Guatemala out of tourist brochures for Punch's special project.

"I thought you were doing Ireland, dear,"

murmured his mother when she came to kiss him goodnight.

After his parents had gone to bed, Howard tiptoed down to the kitchen.

He put a bowl of chocolate chip soup on the table. He put a spoon beside it. And right next to the spoon he placed a bottle of Orange Fizzie.

On the bottle, he taped a note:

Gohst.

This is for you.

He had written "dear gohst," at first, but crossed out the "dear" part. He thought it might make the ghost suspicious.

He left just one light on, the kitchen light.

In the middle of the night, he heard noises again.

Creak. Creak. Thud. Creak. Creak.

Good, he thought, snuggling up against Scruffy Monkey. The ghost's going for it.

Then he heard a different sound.

The toilet flushed.

A tap was turned on.

The ghost was going to the bathroom!

Howard jumped out of bed and raced to his parents' room.

This time he didn't forget Scruffy Monkey.

"Mom! Dad!" he hollered, jumping onto their bed.

They were both in it.

"For pete's sake!" cried Dad. "What is it, Howie?"

"The ghost!" shouted Howard. "It's in the bathroom!"

Mom sat up. She felt Howard's forehead.

"Charles," she said to her husband. "Does he feel feverish to you?"

"He sounds feverish," muttered Dad. He pulled a pillow over his head.

Mom felt Howard's head again. "Okay, dear. You can sleep with us tonight."

"But this is the last time!" said Dad. His voice was very muffled.

In the morning, Howard checked the kitchen while his parents were getting dressed.

The chocolate chip soup bowl was empty.

So was the Orange Fizzie bottle.

"All right!" shouted Howard. His plan was working.

He decided he'd better wash the dishes before his parents saw them.

When he picked up the bowl, he found the note. It said:

> Howie,
>
> Great soup. Next time, please leave Pineapple Fizzie if possible.
>
> Thanks,
> Ghost.

Chapter 8

A Good and Thirsty Ghost

The plan seemed to be working.

Every night, all week, the ghost ate Howard's chocolate chip soup and drank his Pineapple Fizzie.

The ghost seemed to be getting noisier, too. Sometimes, Howard heard a distant *tap, tap, tap*. It sounded like Mom typing away at her magazine job, but she was always asleep when it happened. And whenever the tapping stopped, the floorboards began to creak.

Even his parents noticed it.

"Have you been pottering about at night?" Dad asked Howard.

Howard shook his head.

"I think he's been sleepwalking, Charles," said Mom. "Perhaps we should have him checked out by a doctor."

"He's been doing too much homework," complained Dad. "Look at the circles under his eyes. It's not normal for a kid to do so much homework."

On Thursday, Dad replaced the missing tread on the staircase and painted it. He replaced the Watch Your Step sign with a Wet Paint sign.

Maybe the ghost will leave footprints, thought Howard.

That night, the ghost did not go *creak, creak, thud, creak, creak.* He went, *creak, creak, thud, crash, crash.* But he did not leave any footprints.

On Friday, Howard asked Mom whether he could invite some friends over for a sleepover that weekend. "But Saturday is Halloween," protested Mom. "You'll be out trick-or-treating."

"Please, Mom," pleaded Howard. "It'll be fun. We'll have a costume-party sleepover. Everybody can stay in my room."

Finally, Mom agreed.

Punch said he would come. "Maybe I'll be able to rescue Chokey," he said. He looked sad whenever he spoke of his snake.

Howard ran into trouble with Willie and Rebecca, though.

"You expect me to sleep in the same room as Punch McLaredy?" asked an amazed Willie. "I wouldn't even *sit* in the same room as him if I could help it. He's a bully!"

"He's not so bad," said Howard. "Really, he's pretty nice." He explained about the truce. He didn't mention the homework, though. That was a secret.

"I'm not going to lick sand," said Rebecca.

"Me neither," said Willy. He shook his head as if he thought Howard had gone nuts.

Howard realized he would have to tell his friends about his plan for catching the ghost. He needed their help. There was no telling what kind of a fight the ghost would put up, and he and Punch might not be able to bag him all by themselves.

" . . . so, you see, I really need you," finished Howard.

"Punch let you have his snake?" wondered Willie.

"And he didn't kill you when you lost it?" marvelled Rebecca.

They took a few minutes to think about it. Finally, they agreed to come.

"This might be my only chance to meet a ghost who writes notes," said Rebecca.

"Great," said Howard. "Bring your flashlights. And make sure you wear a really scary costume. We're going to have to be really scary to catch that ghost."

That night, Howard got things ready.

He cooked up a super-delicious, enormous batch of chocolate chip soup. He wanted that ghost to be good and thirsty.

He looked through all the boxes that still hadn't been unpacked until he found his old

Dracula costume and face paints.

He found an old sheet that Mom had been using to catch paint dribbles. He cut holes near the edges and threaded some rope through them. When he pulled on the rope, the sheet gathered into a bag. It was a little difficult to manage, but it was the closest thing to a ghost-catching net that he could make.

Then he did an extra-good job of Punch's book report so that Punch would have to do an extra-good job for him.

He called Punch and got him to agree not to make Willie and Rebecca lick sand.

"How about birdseed?" asked Punch.

"Not even birdseed," replied Howard firmly.

He checked the batteries in his Porky Pig flashlight. And he even poked around with it in some pretty dark and spiderwebby closets, looking for Chokey.

He looked up the phone number for the police and taped it to the telephone in the kitchen.

And finally, just for fun, he helped Dad carve eight jack-o'-lanterns. Enough to line both sides of the stairs to the front door.

This would be the first Halloween in Howard's lifetime that anybody had lived in the brown house on Walnut Street.

Anybody except the ghost, that is.

The jack-o'-lanterns would let everybody know that they could trick-or-treat there.

"Should we hang our plastic skeleton on the door?" wondered Dad. He and Howard were standing out front, admiring their work.

"No, Dad," said Howard. "This house is scary enough already."

Chapter 9

Double Trouble, Boil and Glubble

Saturday evening at seven, three monsters with sleeping bags showed up at Howard's house.

They were very nervous-looking monsters. Even Punch.

"Halloween might not be the best time to catch a ghost," said Willie, as the double door creaked shut behind them. "They might have special powers or something."

"Or he might have relatives visiting. From out of town," said Rebecca.

Howard couldn't see her face behind its

warty, oozy monster mask. But her voice sounded faint.

Punch, who had horns and green skin, was taking a look around for his snake.

"Hey, this place doesn't look half bad," he said, sounding surprised. "You guys should have seen it a week ago."

The brown house on Walnut Street was indeed looking better. It was still old. But with the spiderwebs gone and the wallpaper replaced, it was beginning to look almost cozy.

Just then, Mom walked in, carrying a tray of goodies. She was wearing a black cape and pointy hat.

"Double trouble, boil and glubble," she cackled. "Would you creatures like some witchy treats?"

The monsters took some but Dracula rolled his eyes.

"Everybody knows witches aren't like that," he muttered.

Howard took his friends trick-or-treating around the neighbourhood.

The best stop was Mrs. Merrymore's place.

Mrs. Merrymore was wearing a sparkly orange ballgown and sequined shoes. She had a glittery tiara in her hair and carried a wand with a star-shaped sugar cookie on top.

"This is kind of a special day for me," she smiled.

They were invited in for a special witch feast, and got to sit at a table set with thirty-one orange candles.

"Where's your black cat?" asked Rebecca. She tipped up her mask so that she could try the licorice spaghetti.

"She doesn't have a black cat," said Howard. "She has a white budgie." He smiled at his friend the witch.

"What is this stuff?" asked Punch, sniffing at his tall green drink. "Gizzard guts?"

"Perhaps," said Mrs. Merrymore. "Or perhaps it's gooseberry-dandelion julep."

When they left, she handed each of them a bag. Each bag contained a recipe for chocolate chip soup and a vial of secret soup potion.

Punch got two bags. One had something in it that looked like meatloaf.

"Veggie burger," Mrs. Merrymore said, winking. "For Chokey."

"Has she got a crystal ball?" Punch asked Howard as they hurried to the next house. "How did she know about my snake?"

The worst stop was at Mrs. Nutt's.

She didn't even answer the door, although she was home. Through the window, they could see her TV going.

"She's the real witch," muttered Punch.

Howard would have agreed with him. But that would have been unfair to Mrs. Merrymore.

Back at Howard's house, everything ran smoothly.

Howard's parents went to bed early. They were worn out from all their painting and cleaning to get ready for Gramma.

"Are you all going to sleep in your costumes?" Mom asked when she came to say goodnight.

The monsters were still monsters. And

Howard was still Dracula, except that he'd taken his fangs out. For now.

"We can't change back until after Halloween," said Dracula.

"G-r-r-r," growled Punch, waving his claws in the air.

"All right," said Mom, doubtfully. "Just as long as you don't behave like monsters. Get some sleep."

"We will!" promised the night creatures.

After Howard was sure his parents were asleep, the whole gang tiptoed down to the kitchen.

They found a big mixing bowl and filled it to the brim with soup. Instead of a regular spoon, they put a ladle by the bowl.

Howard taped a note to the bowl. It said,

Dear Gohst,
Happy Halloween. Dig in.
Howie.

This time, it did not feel strange to write "Dear." In a way, Howard was becoming fond of his ghost.

Just as they had planned, Howard did not put out a bottle of Fizzie.

They carried all the bottles of Fizzie upstairs and drank them themselves.

"That's going to be one thirsty ghost," laughed Punch.

Nobody felt much like eating Halloween candy. They were too nervous.

For a while, they played with Howard's fluorescent dominoes. They made a long line of them out the bedroom door and down the hall.

After they had knocked it down and set it up three times, Howard put his finger to his lips.

"Did you hear that?" he whispered.

They all huddled together on Howard's bed. And listened.

Creak. Creak. Creak. Creak. Creak.

"Hey, no thud this time," said Howard.

"What?"

"Nothing."

Creak. Creak. Creak.

There was a pause.

Clackety-clack. Clack-clack-clack.

The dominoes were falling over in the hallway!

One by one, the dominoes in Howard's room fell, too.

Pushed by a ghostly hand!

"Holy macaroni!" said Punch.

Nobody else said anything.

All of a sudden, now that the time had come, Howard didn't feel like going down to the kitchen and catching the ghost. Even with Scruffy Monkey, Punch, Rebecca and Willie beside him.

But he had to.

Chapter 10

Gotcha!

Howard put his fangs back in. If he had to face a ghost, he wanted to look as scary as possible.

He also tucked Scruffy Monkey under his cape.

Just in case.

"I wish I had Chokey right now," said Punch. His voice trembled. Under his green face paint, he didn't look like a bully anymore.

Punch McLaredy looked more like Scaredy McLaredy, thought Howard.

And since Howard knew what it felt like to be

afraid, he knew what to say.

"No matter what," he said, "we stick together. Right, gang?"

"Right!" cried Rebecca, Willie, and Punch.

They huddled together near the door.

The ghost should be just about finished his soup by now, thought Howard.

"Flashlights ready?" he asked.

"Ready!" chorused the monsters.

"Monster masks on?"

"On!"

"Ghost net ready?"

There was a lot of shuffling.

"Don't *you* have it?" asked Punch.

"Oh, yeah," murmured Howard. He reached under his bed and pulled out the net he had made from a sheet. He carried it to the front of the group.

"Forward, march!" called Howard.

The night creatures marched on tiptoes down the stairs.

Punch tapped Howard on the shoulder halfway down.

"I'm sorry I called you Fraidy Brady," he said.

"You're not."

"That's okay." Howard smiled. "Sometimes I am."

And right now he definitely was. Down in the kitchen, waiting for them, was the ghost, thought Howard. A big, fat, glow-in-the-dark ghost. Or a tall, thin, walk-through-the-wall ghost. A ghost who could write. A ghost who could eat.

A ghost who might eat *them!*

Howard wished he could run upstairs with Scruffy Monkey and jump into bed with his parents.

But everybody was looking at him. And counting on him.

Even Punch.

How about that!

Using their flashlights, they found their way to the kitchen. Then they clipped their flashlights to their belts.

The kitchen light was on.

They could hear the ghost.

The fridge squeaked opened, then slammed shut.

Cupboard doors opened, then banged closed, one after another.

Crash! Crash! Crash!

"He's looking for the Pineapple Fizzie!" whispered Howard. The plan was really working.

"We'd better get him before he gets too mad," said Punch.

Each of the ghost hunters took a corner of the ghost net.

Howard looked at his team of monsters.

"Remember," he said solemnly, "if things go wrong, *get my dad!*"

Then he gave the signal, and they charged.

It all happened in a flash. Howard could barely make out a white form — on its knees and peering into a cupboard — before the net was dropped over the ghost.

"We got him!" yelled Punch.

The ghost was struggling to get up.

"Pull the rope!" hollered Howard.

They all yanked.
The ghost landed with a thud on the floor.
"Yahoo!" shouted Rebecca and Willie.
"Hurray!" cried Punch and Howard.
All the ghost said was, "Ow!"

Chapter 11

A Ghost Story

"Untie me!" commanded the ghost.

That didn't sound like the right thing for a ghost to say, thought Howard. A ghost should say *"Aa-woo-oo-oo"* or *"be-e-e go-o-o-one!"* or something like that.

This ghost sounded more like somebody's old uncle.

"Untie me!" said the ghost again, sounding not at all happy. "My elbow hurts."

"You've got to be kidding," said Punch. "After all we've been through!"

Howard untied him anyway.

When the rope was loosened, the monsters stepped back a few steps. Howard lifted the sheet.

Sitting on the floor, rubbing his elbow, was a grey-haired man wearing a white nightgown.

Howard's jaw dropped.

"Who are you?" he asked.

"The ghost," said the man. And grinned.

"Come off it!" said Howard. "You're no ghost."

The ghost looked sad. "Maybe not," he said. "But I wish I was."

Howard helped the ghost into a chair.

"I'll tell you about it," said the ghost, "if you get me some Fizzie. I'm so thirsty!"

Everybody laughed, except Punch. "Where's my snake?" he demanded. "Where's Chokey?"

The ghost squinted at Punch.

"Ah, yes. The window-smasher. While we're wondering where things are, what do you suppose happened to the antique bicycle I used to keep by the back gate?"

Punch didn't say anything. He took a seat far away from the ghost. His ears were standing out more than usual.

Willie found a cup and brought the ghost some water.

The ghost gulped it down.

"That's great chocolate chip soup," he said to Howard. "But it sure keeps you up at night."

"Yeah, I heard you pacing," said Howard. He remembered how the floorboards had creaked over his bed night after night.

The ghost told his story.

"This used to be my house," he said. "Well, not really my house. My grandfather's house. And my father's house. Naturally, I thought it would be my house, too. When I was a boy, seventy years ago, this was a beautiful house. The best in town."

The ghost looked sadly around the kitchen.

"Unfortunately," he said, "my father lost his fortune in the Great Depression. And I didn't turn out to be a rich dentist or gold miner the way he wanted me to. I became a writer."

The ghost took another sip of water.

"Writers can be rich," said Howard.

The ghost raised his eyebrows. "Yes? Well, not me. I write ghost stories. Spooky, chilly ghost stories. But nobody wants them. I haven't sold a story in twenty years," he sighed. "Nobody seems to read ghost stories anymore."

"I do," said Howard. "At least, I read Spook comic books. Does that count?"

The ghost shook his head.

"So, when I couldn't pay the taxes on the house," he said, "the city took it. They kicked me out. Well, I didn't have anywhere else to go. I've been living in the attic ever since."

The ghost looked at Howard. " 'Course, it hasn't been easy since you Bradys moved in," he said. "Can't come and go as I wish. Have to type my stories at night. Even have to wait until everybody is in bed to use the bathroom!"

Howard laughed. Then he thought of something. "How do you get into the attic?" he asked. "I looked. There's no stairs."

"No stairs that you'd notice," said the ghost.

"But if you look very carefully at the ceiling in the hall near your bedroom, you'll see a trapdoor. It's almost hidden by the panelling. It has stairs that fold down. There's a hidden switch on the wall that closes them, too. I knew you'd never catch on!" The ghost chuckled. "I'd unfold the stairs, fold them up behind me, and head straight down to the kitchen!"

"I heard you," said Howard, remembering the creaking. "You used to jump over the missing step."

"Right," said the ghost. "I always liked doing that. Except the one night when I crash-landed." He looked sad again. "I guess I'll have to move out, now that I've been caught."

Rebecca and Willie looked at Howard.

Howard knew what they were thinking.

They wanted him to let the ghost stay.

And so did he. Not every house has a ghost. And not every house has a ghost writer, either.

But Howard knew what his parents would say.

They'd say what parents always say.

No.

"More water, please," asked the ghost.

Howard took his glass over to the sink. He turned on the water.

And turned. And turned. And turned.

At first, nothing happened.

Then there was a trembling in the tap.

A clanging in the pipes.

A thundering in the wall.

The tap handle flew off in Howard's hands and water gushed everywhere.

Over the monsters, over the ghost, across the floor.

The water knocked pots off hooks, vases off shelves, and the lightbulb out of its socket.

"What's going on down there?" hollered Mom from upstairs.

The handle blew off the hot water tap then, too.

"Run for the hills!" screamed Howard.

And Dracula, three monsters, and a ghost raced out the front door.

Chapter 12

A Blood-Curdling Scream

It was cold out on the front lawn.

Cold and dark.

All the candles had burned out in the jack-o'-lanterns, and there was a burnt pumpkin smell in the air.

"Isn't it wonderful?" said the ghost. "I haven't been outside since you moved in." And he did a little jig, clapping the heels of his slippers together.

"We're really in for it now," Howard shivered. Mom and Dad would probably send him to reform school for flooding the kitchen. He could hear a lot of banging and crashing going on in the house. Howard's parents were trying to fix the taps.

There was a time, only a few days before, when Howard might have liked to go to reform school.

But not now. Not now that he had nabbed his ghost.

"You know something," said Rebecca. "You are a pretty brave person, Howard. And a lot more interesting than I thought."

"Yeah," said Willie. "You are the only person in this neighbourhood who is friends with a witch and who lives with an almost-real ghost."

"Hey, ghost!" said Punch, in a cranky voice. "Do you eat snakes?"

The ghost laughed. "No," he said. "But I threw one out the window once."

"Awww," cried Punch, looking pretty upset.

Just then, Howard's parents came out onto the lawn. They were soaking wet.

"It's hopeless, kids," said Dad, wringing out his slippers. "The pipes have blown and the plumber is in Hawaii."

"I know where the main shut-off is," exclaimed the ghost. And he hurried into the house.

"Who's he?" asked Dad. He was jumping up and down on one foot, shaking water out of his ear.

Howard didn't answer. He waited for the ghost to come back.

In a few minutes, the ghost came out again. He was wearing Dad's coat and boots.

"It's off," he said.

"Dad, I'd like you to meet—" began Howard.

"I'm Howard's ghost," said the ghost. He shook Dad's hand. "Warbles is the name. Conrad Warbles."

Dad sat on the stairs. He put his head on his arms.

"It's awfully late for this," he groaned. "Not to mention that I have four kids here, a flooded house, and we're freezing to death."

"Warbles, Warbles," murmured Mom. "Now where have I heard that name?"

She paced back and forth, her wet slippers flapping. Then she spun on one heel and pointed at the ghost.

"You're Conrad Warbles the writer!" she exclaimed. "I used to read your stuff when I was a kid. You write great ghost stories!"

Warbles the ghost bowed.

"At your service," he said. He seemed pleased.

Howard told Mom and Dad the ghost's story.

"You're the one who's been using my typewriter!" said Mom. "I thought it was Howard, sleepwalking!"

"It seems a shame that we've bought your house," said Dad. "But we can't give it back, you know. Where would we go?"

"Charles, do you think . . . ?" asked Mom.

She pulled Dad over to a tree and they whispered together.

When they came back, they were smiling.

"Would you like to stay on with us?" asked

Dad. "We need someone to keep an eye on the pipes, keep Gramma company when she comes, things like that."

"And I could really use some ghost stories for my magazine," said Mom. "I'm the editor of Commas & Dots. I've often thought of looking you up, but since I never saw any of your stories any more, I thought you were — "

"Dead?" laughed Conrad Warbles. "Not dead. Just a little ghostly, that's all."

At that moment, a blood-curdling scream came from Mrs. Nutt's house.

Everybody dashed over there.

The door flew open and Mrs. Nutt tumbled out.

"There's a snake in there!" she screamed. "A slithery, withery, woman-eating snake. It got my cane!"

"Chokey!" yelled Howard and Punch.

They raced into Mrs. Nutt's house. Down the hallway. Up the stairs. Through the study and into the bedrooms.

There was no sign of Chokey.

"He's gone again!" wailed Punch.

"Wait!" said Howard. "Where's your snake food?"

Punch found it in his pocket.

Howard found Mrs. Nutt's cane lying in her bedroom. He squished some veggie burger onto the end of it.

"Here, Chokey, Chokey," he called, pushing the cane into dark corners and under furniture.

He couldn't believe he, Howard the Coward, was really calling a snake!

In a few minutes, the snake followed the cane out from under a dresser.

Punch stuffed Chokey into a pillowcase and gave the pillowcase a big hug. He did not look the least bit like a bully.

"Thanks," he said to Howard. "You're not a yo-yo after all. And I guess you don't have to do my homework anymore. Your marks weren't so great, anyway."

Mrs. Nutt was so grateful that she made tea and served butterscotch biscuits in her dining

room, not minding that everyone was soaking wet.

She turned out to be pretty nice after all. Even if she didn't believe in Halloween.

When she heard about their plumbing disaster, she shook her head at Howard's mom. "I warned you that old house would be trouble, Charlene." Then she smiled. "But I'm glad you didn't listen."

After the three monsters and Dracula, all dried off and changed back into their regular selves, had climbed into bed, Howard heard a familiar noise.

Creak. Creak. Creak. Tap-tap-tappety-tap.

The ghost was home. Writing another ghost story.

"Well," said Howard, drowsily. His tummy was full of butterscotch biscuits and he felt warm and cozy.

As he lay there, he whispered to himself: "I'm still afraid of some things. I'm afraid of spiders, some creaky noises, and the dark. I'm not too sure about snakes yet.

"But there's three things I'm not afraid of. Witches. Bullies. And ghosts.

"How many people can say that?"

Maureen Bayless

Even with three boys and various foster children (not to mention several squirrel families living in her attic), Maureen Bayless somehow finds time to write, and has even managed to keep her sense of humour.

Maureen and her family live in Vancouver, where she is working on several other books.